PAINTBALL
PROBLEMS

BY ERIC STEVENS
ILLUSTRA...

STONE
a capstone imprint

Jake Maddox books are published by Stone Arch Books
A Capstone Imprint
1710 Roe Crest Drive
North Mankato, Minnesota 56003
www.capstonepub.com

Library of Congress Cataloging-in-Publication Data
Maddox, Jake.
  Paintball problems / by Jake Maddox ; text by Eric Stevens ; illustrated by
Jesus Aburto.
     p. cm. -- (Jake Maddox sports stories)
  Summary: Sixth-grader Max Stinson is tired of being bullied by Alex
Weime and looking forward to a summer in the local paintball league to
work off some of his frustration, but he soon learns that anger is not a
winning attitude, especially when you take it out on the people around you.
  ISBN 978-1-4342-5974-5 (library binding) -- ISBN 978-1-4342-6207-3 (pbk.)
1. Paintball (Game)--Juvenile fiction. 2. Bullying--Juvenile fiction. 3.
Anger--Juvenile fiction. [1. Paintball (Game)--Fiction. 2. Bullies--Fiction.
3. Anger--Fiction. 4. Emotions--Fiction.] I. Stevens, Eric, 1974- II. Aburto,
Jesus, ill. III. Title. IV. Series: Maddox, Jake. Impact books. Jake Maddox
sports story.
  PZ7.M25643Pil 2013
  813.6--dc23

                              2012049365

Art Director: Bob Lentz
Graphic Designer: Veronica Scott
Production Specialist: Laura Manthe

Printed in the United States of America in Stevens Point, Wisconsin.
032013   007227WZF13

TABLE OF CONTENTS

CHAPTER 1

LAST DAY

Max Stinson hit the ground hard and got a mouthful of mud. Over the sound of his own coughing, he heard mean laughter.

"Have a good trip, Max," a nasty voice said from above him. "See you next fall!"

Max looked up and saw Alex Werme, the biggest, meanest boy in the sixth grade. His goons were with him too. Each of them would have been happy to be the school bully if Alex hadn't claimed the title.

Max stayed where he was. Whevener Alex was around, Max always seemed to end up in a mud puddle.

"See ya, Max," Alex added as he lightly kicked Max's shoulder. As he walked away, Alex muttered, "Sooner than you think."

Pulling himself up onto his knees, Max saw his best friend, Owen Juele, walking toward him. Max and Owen had grown up on the same block and spent every afternoon after school together. Both of Owen's parents worked full time, so they always went to Max's house.

Owen came to a stop next to Max. He made sure to keep his sneakers just out of the mud puddle.

"Come on," Owen said. He held out his hand. "They're gone."

"Thanks a lot," said Max. "You could have helped me before they tripped me into the mud."

"Then I would have ended up in the mud too," said Owen. "Sounds like a bad idea."

Max grunted and climbed to his feet, knocking Owen's hand away. "Some friend you are," he said.

Suddenly, he spotted something that made him forget all about Owen. His backpack — packed full of all the junk he'd finally cleaned out of his locker — was sitting in the mud, soaked.

"Oh, no," Max said. "My mom is going to kill me."

"Yeah," said Owen. "Probably."

Max sighed and grabbed his bag. "Let's just get out of here," he grumbled.

"Hey," said Owen, patting his friend on the shoulder. "At least the paintball league starts tomorrow. That'll give you something to look forward to."

"Maybe Alex and his friends will join," said Max with a sneer. "I'd love to cover all of them with splotches of paint."

He wiped mud off the face of his watch and checked the time. "Speaking of the league, we'd better hurry," he said. "Sign-ups already started."

With that, the boys climbed on their bikes and headed off.

CHAPTER 2

PAINTBALL LEAGUE

Max and Owen skidded to a stop in front of Splat Arena. A big sign above the arena's two front doors read: SUMMER YOUTH PAINTBALL LEAGUE SIGN-UPS TODAY.

"I thought this summer would never get here," Max said as they hurried inside.

There were about twenty kids standing around. Max nodded at the college-aged guy leaning on the sign-up counter and smiling. "Look," Max said. "It's Jace."

Jace Jennings had once been the best player in the youth paintball league. Now he volunteered as a team leader. The previous summer, he'd led the yellow team to the league championship.

"Do you think he'll be our team leader again this summer?" Max asked.

"I hope so," Owen said. "He's the best coach here."

"Hey, guys," Jace said as Max and Owen walked up to the sign-up line. "Joining the yellow team again, I hope?"

"Definitely!" Max said. "We'll have the best coach again, right?"

"You know it," Jace said with a laugh. "You guys get signed up. I'll make sure you're both on my team. See you tomorrow for the first day."

Max and Owen eventually reached the front of the line. They picked up rules pamphlets and permission slips for their parents to sign, then headed for the exit.

But Max didn't quite make it there — at least, not on his feet. As he walked out the front door, he tripped over something and landed on the grass with a *thud!*

"Ow," Max said, groaning. He rolled over and saw Alex standing over him.

"Another nice trip for Max," Alex said. He stopped next to Max on the lawn. His goon friends stood behind him, laughing.

"What's Max short for, anyway?" Alex continued. "Maximum Dork?"

Max didn't respond. He just waited for Alex to finish making fun of him and move on. Finally, the bully and his friends left.

Max sat up. "Thanks for helping," he said to Owen. "Again."

Owen offered Max help getting up, but Max slapped his hand away.

"Look at it this way," Owen said. "Sure, he's a bully, and he's tripped you twice today and made you look like a fool and got you covered in mud and grass stains —"

"What's your point?" Max interrupted. He gritted his teeth and stood up.

"My point is, you got your wish," Owen said. "If he's here to sign up for the paintball league, you'll be able to cover him with yellow paint, just like you wanted."

Max grunted. "Alex thinks I'll make an easy target," he said. "I just hope he's wrong."

CHAPTER 3

THE SCRIMMAGE

Right after breakfast the next morning, Owen and Max jumped on their bikes and took off for Splat Arena. Jace and the other team leaders, along with Stan, the league manager, were the only ones there when Max and Owen arrived.

"You guys are early," Stan said.

"We were too excited to sleep!" Max said.

"Good to hear. But remember, we're just scrimmaging today," Stan reminded them.

"I know," Max said. "The coaches need to see what they're dealing with."

"And you kids need some practice," Jace said with a grin. "Most of you haven't been in matches in almost a year."

"Owen and I have," Max said. He ran his finger along the barrel of a yellow-team marker. "We were in the winter league while you were away at college."

"I said 'most,'" said Jace. "Now grab a jumpsuit and get ready to scrimmage."

* * *

Thirty minutes later, everyone else had arrived and gotten dressed for the scrimmage. Stan gathered all the players and went over the rules.

This is taking forever, Max thought. *I just want to start already.*

"Today's scrimmage will feature two teams with four players each," Stan said. "We'll put new players in when someone on the field is eliminated. Everyone will get plenty of play time."

Stan went on, "Grab a marker, but don't fill your hopper yet. You'll get paintballs when you rotate in. Let's play!"

"Finally," Max whispered to Owen. "I thought we'd never get to play."

Owen smirked and pulled down the goggles of his mask. "Let's get this show on the road," he said in a gruff voice.

Owen was picked as one of the first eight players on the field. Max and the others moved to the observation area to watch.

"Make sure to stay lined up so we know who rotates in next," Jace reminded them.

Someone shoved Max from behind. "Oops," Alex muttered.

Great. He's right after me, Max thought. *That means we'll almost definitely be playing at the same time.*

Max watched as the teams moved onto the field. Down below, the ground was covered with obstacles, mounds of dirt, and plastic barrels.

The other players hid among the shields and barricades in the middle of the field, no-man's land. Max watched Owen move around the back, staying low. No one spotted him until he had his marker up and an opposing player in his sights.

Owen managed to mark two players on the other team. He hit the ground to avoid being eliminated as the players fired back.

"Nice going, Owen!" Max shouted.

"Next two in," Stan shouted. "Load up with red, please."

The two boys in front of Max hurried to fill their hoppers. Then they entered the arena behind the red team's barricades. There, they would be safe for a few seconds as the scrimmage continued.

Max shuffled forward. He was next.

Jace put a hand on his shoulder. "Remember, this is just a scrimmage," he said. "No winners or losers. Just play."

"I know," Max said. He pulled down his goggles. Owen was in midfield now and sitting with his back against a plastic barrel. He was playing a slow style. He'd sit and wait for an opportunity to mark the other team. That way he avoided a shootout.

Meanwhile, another player on Owen's team ran across no-man's land, firing wildly at the red team. He missed with every one. But one red paintball struck his arm.

"Eliminated!" Stan called over the loudspeaker.

Jace gave Max a friendly shove. "Get in there," he said.

Max grinned and loaded his hopper with blue paintballs. He sprinted onto the blue side of the field, making sure to stay well hidden. Stooped behind some green netting, Max raised his marker. He spotted a member of the red team, aimed, and fired.

"Eliminated!" shouted Stan. "Next player, red team."

Max looked up at the waiting area. Alex stood there, grinning from ear to ear.

CHAPTER 4

BULLIES IN THE GAME

Alex played exactly like Max had expected him to. He barreled across the field, counting on the blue team's poor aim and slow markers to keep him clean. He sprinted toward the blue side of the field, heading straight for Max.

Max was forced to flee. But he was a crafty player and stayed low, finding a good hiding place. From there, he watched Alex stomp through the field, ignoring the rest of the blue team.

Owen took advantage of Alex's focus and aggression. He managed to mark two members of the red team while Max hid.

"Next two players," Stan called out.

Max kept his eyes on Alex. The big bully still hadn't found him. Alex stalked across no-man's land, intent on hunting Max down.

Max smiled. He almost laughed. A few more steps, and he'd would have a clear shot. He could mark Alex easily.

For a moment, Alex stepped out of sight behind a pair of barrels. As he did, Max realized something. Even though no one on the field could see him, the players up in the observation area could. And two of them had just entered the field to join the red team — Alex's friends.

I need a better hiding place, Max thought frantically.

But it was too late. The moment he tried to sneak away, Alex's two friends were there blocking his way.

"Wait a second," Alex shouted, running over. "Maximum Dork is mine."

As he got closer, Alex lifted his marker, pointed it straight at Max's helmet, and squeezed the trigger.

Splat!

CHAPTER 5

FOUL!

Whistles blew. Stan shouted from the observation area, "Foul! Foul!"

Max could hardly hear it. The bang of the paintball against his helmet had left a ringing in his head. "Ow," he said.

Jace came running across the field toward them. "Alex!" he shouted. "The rules require a minimum marking distance of fifteen feet. You could have really hurt Max."

"Oh, sorry," Alex said with a smirk. He didn't sound sorry at all. "I'm used to rules at a different arena. I didn't know there were special rules for Maximum Dork."

"Get off the field," Jace said. "You're on the bench the rest of the day."

Alex just laughed as he headed off the field. Jace knelt down beside Max.

"Are you okay?" he said.

"I think so," Max said. His hearing was starting to come back.

"Well, that was an illegal mark, obviously," Jace said. "So if you're feeling okay, you can stay in the match."

"I'm fine," Max insisted.

"So, I'm guessing you and Alex didn't meet for the first time today," Jace said.

Max shrugged. "He's in my class at school," he said.

"Does he pick on you a lot?" Jace asked, looking concerned. "Do you want to talk?"

"No," Max said quickly.

"Well, I'll be keeping an eye on him," Jace said. Finally, he stood up and headed back to the observation area.

I wish he'd back off, Max thought. *I don't need him to make me look like more of a baby.*

Max got to his feet and took a deep breath. He didn't even take cover as play started again. He just ran into the middle of the field, shooting off paintballs like crazy and marking members of the red team.

When the scrimmage time was over, Max was still on the field, red-faced and breathing hard.

"Good work out there," Owen said as Max came off the field.

But Max hardly heard him. He was too busy watching Alex and his bully friends cackling as they turned in their gear. He couldn't hear what they were saying, but he could guess. They were laughing at him.

How dare they laugh at me! Max thought furiously. *I probably got the most eliminations all day. I was on the field the longest.*

Max stomped up to the counter to turn in his gear as Alex and his friends headed toward the exit.

Jerks. I'll teach them, Max thought.

Just then, someone tapped Max on the shoulder. He spun around, his face red and his hands balled into fists. "What?!" he yelled.

It was Owen. "Um, you okay?" he said, looking startled. "Jace and I have been calling your name for like five minutes."

"I'm fine," Max snapped. He stalked toward the exit. "Let's just get out of here."

* * *

Max didn't speak to Owen at all on the bike ride home. When he reached his house, his little sister, Deedee, was out front drawing on the sidewalk with chalk.

"Watch out, nerd," Max barked. He skidded to a stop inches from her.

"Hey! You're messing up my picture," Deedee said. She stood up and faced the front door. "Mom!"

"Mom!" said Max in a snotty imitation. "Don't be such a baby, Deedee."

"Stop it!" his sister shouted at him.

Max got off his bike and shoved his sister. Deedee fell back onto her butt on the grass. She looked up at him, her eyes big and wet. Then she screamed.

Great, Max thought. *Now I'm going to be in trouble on top of everything else.*

He hurried to push his bike into the garage and dropped it against the wall. Then he went into the house, ran straight to up to his room, and slammed the door.

CHAPTER 6

THE FIRST MATCH

On the second day of paintball league, the tournament began. Max and Owen found Jace waiting for them beneath the yellow team's banner when they arrived.

"Hey, guys," said Jace. "Here you go." He handed them matching yellow jerseys. "A little nicer than last summer, huh?"

Max nodded. The jerseys were yellow and looked like racing suits.

"Turn them around," Jace said, grinning.

Max turned his jersey over. On the back was a number and his last name, STINSON, in bold, black lettering.

"Awesome!" Max said. "Do we get to keep these?"

Jace nodded. "Yup," he said. "Included in your league entry fee."

"Hey, Max!" a voice yelled.

Max didn't even have to look. It was Alex. He'd know that jerk's voice anywhere.

"Looks like they forgot to put your real last name on your jersey," Alex continued. "You know, Maximum Dork!"

Alex and his bully friends laughed like it was the funniest thing they'd ever heard. They made their way to the green banner.

"Looks like the green team will be our arch nemesis this summer, huh?" said Jace.

Max nodded.

"But not today," said Jace. "Today we face the blue team on field two."

"I wish we were playing the green team today," Max grumbled they made their way to one of the two fields. "I can't wait to show Alex how much better I am."

Jace patted him on the back. "Use that energy to help us win today," he said.

Max nodded. He and Owen took their positions on the field and looked up at Stan in the observation area. Jace stood next to him, signaling to the other players, helping them find good places to start the match.

Finally, Stan put up his hand and blew his whistle. The matches began!

Max took off running. As he darted across the field, shooting his marker wildly, all he could think about was getting revenge on Alex, even though Alex wasn't in the game.

Max ran up one side of the field, his marker in front of him, and shot paintball after paintball into the blue team.

Max's rapid firing left plenty of yellow paint splattered on the obstacles — the barrels and hunks of wood and fake trees. But not a single blue player was eliminated.

Max hardly paid attention to Owen and the other two players on his team. They stayed back, waiting for an opportunity to mark a blue player.

Above him, Jace waved wildly, trying to get his attention. Max didn't care.

He's just going to tell me to play more carefully, Max thought. *What good is that going to do?*

Just then, Max felt a stinging thud against his upper arm. He dropped to the ground and looked at his shoulder. Blue paint.

He was out.

* * *

After the match, Owen — the last yellow player eliminated — found Max sulking in the observation area.

"What was that all about?" Owen said. "You were playing terribly. I've never seen you eliminated so quickly. You okay?"

Max glared at him. "I'm fine," he said as he stood up. "Leave me alone, okay?"

Max stomped off. As he went to the front to turn in his gear for the day, a couple of members of the blue team walked by. They were smiling and laughing about their win.

Max recognized the smallest player from school. He was a short sixth grader.

"What are you laughing about?" Max said. He shoved the kid hard, so that the smaller boy stumbled into the wall.

"Hey," the kid snapped. "What's your problem?"

Max ignored him and dropped his marker and gear at the front table. When he got outside, Owen grabbed his shoulder.

"That wasn't cool," Owen said.

"He was in my way," Max said. Then, without waiting for Owen, he got on his bike and rode off.

CHAPTER 7

A BAD NIGHT

At dinner that night, Max kept his elbows on the table and leaned on one fist. He pushed his rice around the plate and didn't touch his chicken. Across the table, Deedee poked holes in her peanut butter and jelly sandwich.

"I don't see why she gets that and I have to eat this," Max muttered.

"Because I don't eat chicken," Deedee said.

"Yeah, because you're a baby," Max said.

"Mom!" Deedee shrieked.

"That's enough," Dad said. "Both of you, knock it off. Eat your dinner."

Max shoved his plate away. "She's being disgusting," he said, pointing at Deedee's smooshed sandwich. "Tell her to stop being such a disgusting baby."

"That's it," his mom said. "You're done. Go to your room."

"Fine," Max said. His chair fell backward as he stood up. He hurried upstairs without picking it up.

Max slumped in his desk chair and picked up his cell phone. He'd gotten it for his thirteenth birthday and mostly used it to text back and forth with Owen.

I'M THINKING ABOUT QUITTING PAINTBALL, he typed to his friend.

HA HA, Owen replied. VERY FUNNY.

I'M SERIOUS, Max typed back.

WHATEVER. SEE YOU TOMORROW, Owen replied.

Max tossed his phone onto his nightstand and flopped back against his pillow.

CHAPTER 8

TOO FAR

The next morning, Max was feeling a little better. Neither he nor Owen mentioned their text conversation from the night before as they biked to the arena. By the time they arrived, Max was in a pretty good mood.

But it didn't last. As Max locked up his bike, a big black SUV pulled up. Three big guys climbed out of the back seat — Alex and his friends.

As the truck drove away, Alex strode right over to the Max and Owen.

"Well, if it isn't Maximum Dork and his sidekick," he said. "You better hope it's not yellow versus green today. Because if it is, you're both getting pounded."

Owen looked at his feet. Max gritted his teeth and stared at Alex.

"Ooh, look who's tough," Alex said. He and his friends laughed meanly.

"Let's just go, Max," said Owen.

"Just a minute," Alex said. His friends grabbed Max by the arms. Alex gave Max a little slap on the face.

"Let him go, Alex," Owen said.

"In a minute, I said," Alex snarled. He wasn't smiling anymore.

Max didn't speak. He was scared, but he was also angrier than he'd ever been.

Alex looked Max square in the face, pulled back his arm, and punched him in the stomach. His friends released him, and Max fell to the cement. Alex and his friends smirked and walked inside.

Max clutched his stomach. For a few seconds, he thought he might puke.

"I'm going to get Jace," Owen said.

"No," Max gasped, struggling to catch his breath. "I'm fine. He just . . . he just knocked the wind out of me."

"More like he knocked the snot out of you," Owen said. He put out his hand to help him up. For once, Max took it.

"You need to tell Jace," Owen said. "All three of them should be kicked out."

"Then that would only leave one member on the green team," Max said. "They'd have to eliminate the whole team. Everyone would hate me."

"I doubt it," Owen said. "No one likes those guys anyway."

They stepped inside and saw the green team gathered around their team leader. They were huddled together, laughing and planning for their day's match.

"They seem pretty popular to me," Max said.

"If you won't tell," Owen said, "I will."

Max grabbed him by the shirt collar. "If you do, I'll never speak to you again," he said. "Just mind your own business, okay?"

CHAPTER 9

SEEING RED

The yellow team's match that day was against the red team. The moment the match started, Max sprinted into the middle of the field, firing paintballs wildly. This time he managed to hit a red player on the leg, scoring an elimination.

But as he dove for cover next to Owen, the remaining members of the red team bombarded Max. In an instant, he and Owen were covered in red paint.

"Nice going," Owen said as he and Max left the field. "Your insane playing style not only got you eliminated in under thirty seconds, but it got me eliminated too."

Max just shrugged and sat on a bench in the observation area. Owen stood by the window next to Jace to watch the rest of the match. Max found he didn't care at all.

* * *

The yellow team lost their match, but the green team won. Afterward, Alex and his friends came running into the observation area, laughing and high-fiving. Alex spotted Max, sitting alone.

"Hey, Maximum Loser," Alex said. "I hear you were on the field for almost twenty-five seconds today. Must be your new record, huh?"

Max glared furiously as Alex and his friends laughed and laughed.

A member of the red team standing nearby laughed too. He was young, and smaller than Max, but Max was angry. He jumped to his feet and charged the kid, knocking him back into the wall.

The boy in red charged back. He shoved Max, sending him to the floor of the observation area.

Max was sprawled on the floor. Alex and his friends gathered around and laughed even harder.

CHAPTER 10

A TALKING-TO

After dinner that evening, Max lay on his bed and stared at the ceiling.

"Knock, knock," said Max's dad. He stuck his head in the door. "Got a minute?"

Max didn't answer. *What's the point?* he thought. *It's not like I can say no.* He was pretty sure his dad was going to lecture him about something.

"Deedee was just in the living room," Dad said. "She's pretty upset."

"So?" Max said. "She's always upset about something."

"Well, right now she's upset about how you've been treating her," Dad said.

"She's a tattletale," Max said.

"It's not okay for you to push her around and pick on her," Dad said. "How would you like it if some bigger boy pushed you around all the time?"

"I wouldn't," Max said. He took a deep breath. "I don't." He didn't mean to say anything, but suddenly everything about Alex and his friends, the school year, and the paintball league all came pouring out.

"Why didn't you tell me sooner?" Dad asked when Max had finished talking.

"I didn't want to be a tattletale," Max said. "I figured he'd get bored eventually."

"But he hasn't," Dad said.

"No," Max agreed. "He's gotten worse." He told him about the last thing Alex had done — the big punch in the stomach. "Owen said I should tell on him."

"Owen was right," Dad said.

"I know," said Max.

Dad stood up. "Well, I've got a phone call to make, I think," he said.

"Wait, what?" said Max.

"Your team leader," Dad said. "Same guy as last year, right? His name's Jace, isn't it?"

"Dad, don't call him," Max said.

"Max, I have to. Someday you'll understand," Dad said, leaving the room.

"Great," said Max, falling back again onto his bed. "I'm dead."

CHAPTER 11

SORRY

The next day, Owen and Max were the first kids to arrive at the arena. Jace and Stan were standing off to the side, talking in hushed tones.

When Jace spotted Max and Owen, he quit talking and waved hello. He smiled at them as he walked over.

"Get geared up, guys," he said. "Big match today." He glanced over at Stan. "We're up against the green team."

Soon, Max and Owen stood near the entrance to field one with their markers in their hands and their hoppers loaded.

Across the field, Max could see the members of the green team, ready and waiting to start. But nothing happened. In fact, Stan wasn't even up in the observation area yet.

Owen elbowed Max. "Look," Owen said, pointing across the field. The biggest member of the green team was being pulled away — Alex.

"What's going on?" Max said quietly. Jace and Stan were leading Alex around the field toward the yellow team's entrance.

A moment later, Alex stood in front of him. Jace and Stan were beside him. Alex lifted his goggles and held out his hand.

"I'm sorry for picking on you a little," Alex said. He shoved his hand toward Max.

Max stared at the bully's hand for a moment. Alex cleared his throat. "You're supposed to shake it," he said, a snotty tone in his voice.

Max looked at Stan and Jace. They both nodded a little. Max had no choice. He shook Alex's hand, just for a second. Then Alex turned and walked off.

Stan left to get up to the observation area and start the matches.

"That's the end of that," Jace said. He smiled and patted Max on the back. Then he turned and headed to the observation area too.

"Yeah, right," Owen said. "There's no way that was a sincere apology."

Max shrugged and smiled. "To be honest, I don't even care if it was," he said. "I feel better anyway."

"Why?" Owen said.

Max thought for a moment. "Because I told my dad about it," he said. "It felt good to get it off my chest instead of keeping it bottled up inside." He grinned at Owen. "Now let's focus on what's important," he said. "Let's play some paintball."

CHAPTER 12

KEEPING COOL

Finally, it was time for the players to enter the field. Stan held up one hand and blew his whistle. The match began.

Max took a deep breath. He thought about how angry he'd been the past few days. He thought about the sixth grader he'd shoved. He remembered the red-team member he'd picked on. He thought about Deedee too and how she'd cried in their yard when Max had pushed her down.

And he remembered how he'd felt whenever Alex picked on him. Max wasn't proud of his behavior. He knew he couldn't let a bully turn him into a bully. It was time to focus on what he loved — paintball.

Max stayed crouched on the yellow side of the field. He saw Owen about twenty yards away with his back to a barrel. Max nodded at him, and Owen nodded back.

The two boys moved slowly, staying behind cover. They slid along the side of the field, staying low. Before long, Max lost sight of Owen, but they were a team. They both knew the plan.

Max stayed as low as he could while still on his feet. At the same time, Max and Owen crossed into no-man's land. Max looked up at Jace and waited for the signal.

Around him, Max heard the *thwap* and *splat* of markers and paintballs. No one called an elimination, though, which meant both teams were still full.

Max kept his eyes on Jace and waited. Suddenly, Jace flashed a thumbs-up. It was so quick that anyone else might have missed the signal.

Max darted from his cover, deep into the green side of the field. The green team had their backs to him. Max caught a glimpse of Owen as his friend rushed in from the other side. Together, they raised their markers and squeezed the triggers.

Splat! Splat! Splat! Splat!

"What a play!" Stan yelled "The yellow team's teamwork pays off in a big way with that surprise ambush! Way to go, guys!"

AUTHOR BIO

Eric Stevens lives in St. Paul, Minnesota. He is studying to become a middle-school English teacher. Some of his favorite things include pizza, playing video games, watching cooking shows on TV, riding his bike, and trying new restaurants. Some of his least favorite things include olives and shoveling snow.

ILLUSTRATOR BIO

Aburtov has worked in the comic book industry for more than 11 years. In that time, he has illustrated popular characters like Wolverine, Iron Man, Blade, and the Punisher. He lives in Monterrey, Mexico, with his daughter, Ilka, and his beloved wife.

GLOSSARY

barricade (BA-ruh-kade) — a barrier to stop people from getting past a certain point

crafty (KRAF-tee) — skilled at tricking other people

eliminated (i-LIM-uh-nay-tid) — removed from competition by defeat

league (LEEG) — a group of people with a common interest or activity, such as a group of sports teams

observation (ob-zur-VAY-shuhn) — the careful watching of someone or something

opportunity (op-ur-TOO-nuh-tee) — a chance to do something

scrimmage (SKRIM-ij) — a game played for practice in sports

DISCUSSION QUESTIONS

1. Do you think Alex's apology was real? Talk about your opinion.

2. What are some other ways to deal with bullying? Talk about some different solutions.

3. Why do you think Alex and his friends were so mean to Max? Talk about some possible reasons.

WRITING PROMPTS

1. Write about what you would have done if you were in Max's postition and found out Alex had joined the paintball league.

2. What do you think happens when Max and Alex go back to school after the summer paintball league? Write a chapter that continues this book.

3. Have you ever had to deal with a bully, either in school or somewhere else? Write about how you handled it.

PAINTBALL SAFETY

Paintball can be a lot of fun, but like any sport, there are important safety rules you should follow and safety gear you need to wear while playing.

Safety Gear:

- Face mask — the most important piece of safety equipment; a face mask or helmet is required to play

- Chest and throat protectors — harder to move in, but good protection against bruises

- Barrel plug — every paintball gun should come with a barrel plug that fits snugly on the end of your barrel

- Gloves — useful for protecting your hands while crawling on the ground

Safety Tips:

- Make sure your gear is in good shape before stepping foot on the field.

- Always wear your face mask or goggles whenever you're on the playing field.

- Always keep your paintball gun aimed down toward the ground when you're not playing.

- Never point your paintball gun at someone's face, and don't look into the barrel.

- Always keep your barrel plug in place when you're not on the playing field, and put it on before removing your mask.